D1598081

For
the Hooksett
Library in my
new hometown!
May we get to know each
other well :)

Benen

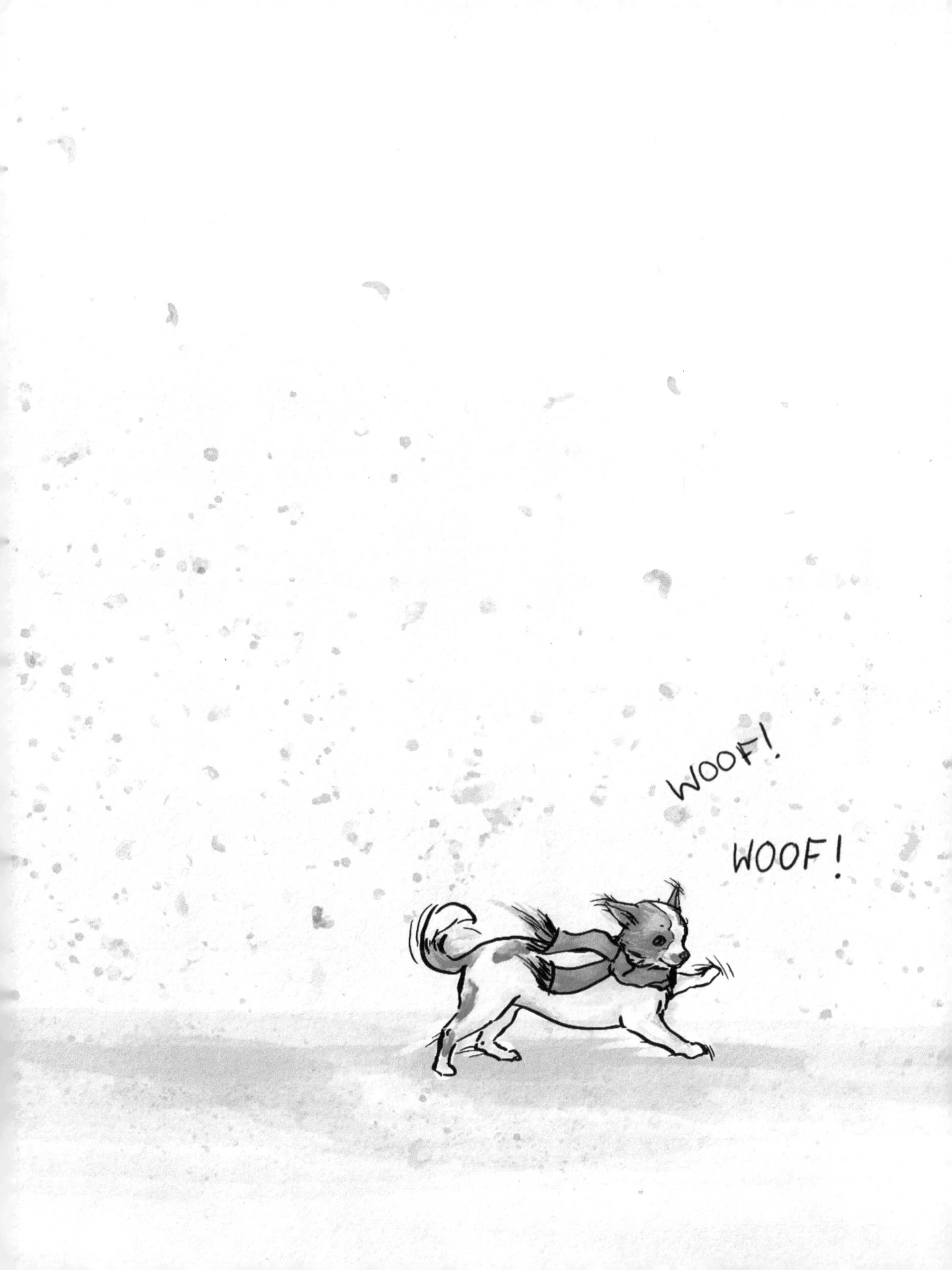
WOOF!
WOOF!

For Eric

A Million More Kisses

René Schultz
&
Becky Stout

"**Geronimo**, get ready to meet **Nonnie!**"
I said excitedly. "We're going to have a
great day!"

Geronimo was **tiny.** His eyes followed the stairs
all
    the
        way
           down
                to the big, red door. "**Woof!**" *It's too far!*

"Come on, boy! **Slow** and **easy**, you'll be **safe**!"

One by one, Geronimo **hopped** down each step.

"**WOOF! WOOF!**" *I did it!*

"**Great job, buddy!**"
I assured him.

Geronimo could **not** stop sniffing!

Nonnie's house had yellow daffodils and a lilac bush.

Did Geronimo hear a squirrel?

Everyone got **excited** when Geronimo walked through the door.

"Everyone, this is Geronimo, I just adopted him!" I said. "He is afraid of loud noises and new people, please be **gentle**."

Some cousins whispered, "Come here, Geronimo!"

Some yelled, "HE'S **SO CUTE!**"

Amidst all the voices, **one** stood out. "Well, hello there, little fella! Did you come to visit Nonnie?"

Geronimo ran to the gentle voice. Sitting in a chair, snuggling a blanket, was a little, elderly woman with gray hair and sparkling eyes. "Come on," she cooed, "Nonnie won't hurt you."

"**WOOF! WOOF!**" Geronimo wagged his tail as Nonnie scooped him up.

"Look at your tongue sticking out!" Nonnie giggled. Her soft touch felt nice as she petted his belly.

"**It's time to go home now!**" I called.

Geronimo hid his nose under Nonnie's blanket. **He didn't want to leave!**

"We will share a special day, soon," Nonnie promised.

Geronimo was able to visit Nonnie **often**.

Together they picked out flowers for her front porch. **Orange**, **red**, and **yellow** chrysanthemums, the colors of autumn!

The New England weather slowly turned cold. The **red** and **yellow** leaves fell off the trees. Soon, it was **Halloween**.

Geronimo helped Nonnie make a scarecrow
wreath for the front door. Outside on the
deck, they carved a pumpkin!

"First, we remove all the seeds," Nonnie explained, "then we carve a smiley
face!" She placed a small candle inside. "See how it glows!"

"Geronimo, come here, boy!" I called. "It's time for trick or treating!"

Geronimo put on his alligator costume and ran to show Nonnie.
"WOOF! WOOF!" *I wonder if Nonnie will recognize me!*

WOOF!
WOOF

"Oh, no!" Nonnie exclaimed, as Geronimo ran into the room. "It's a

big,

scary

ALLIGATOR!"

"WOOF! WOOF!" *It's just me!* He thought. Geronimo didn't mean to scare Nonnie!

"I was just playing," Nonnie chuckled. "Here is a special treat, just for you!"

"WOOF! WOOF!" *Nonnie isn't scared!* That made Geronimo happy.

Every Christmas, Nonnie brought Geronimo to the pet store. They picked out a warm coat and a snuggly, new bed for their slumber parties.

Saturdays in spring
were special.

"Geronimo, grab your coat," Nonnie called.
"We're going to the Kelley Library!"

Audrey, the librarian, handed Nonnie their new books. "Have fun with
your reading!"

"WOOF! WOOF!"
Geronimo **loved** the library!

On hot summer days, Nonnie read to Geronimo by the stream.

He **rolled** in the grass among the purple and yellow wildflowers.

"Peep! Peep!" said a blue jay as it landed close by.

"Caw! Caw!" called the big, black crows as they circled overhead.

"What do you think they're trying to tell us, Geronimo?" Nonnie asked.

Geronimo didn't answer. His tongue hung down as he **slept** under the sun.

One day, Geronimo realized his summer was **different**.
Nonnie didn't sit with him in the wildflowers by the stream,
and he missed seeing Audrey at the library.

"Sorry, buddy," we explained.
"No more car rides with Nonnie."

Finally, one Saturday morning, Geronimo went to Nonnie's for his usual visit.

"Hey, little fella, what are you doing here?" Nonnie asked.

Geronimo stopped in his tracks! His eyes flew open.

"WOOF! WOOF!"

he tried to tell her.

Don't you remember it's Saturday? Why aren't you picking me up to cuddle?

These things **bothered** him as he plopped himself down in his bed, which was now old and worn.

New voices startled Geronimo at the front door!

"WOOF! WOOF!" Geronimo barked, protectively. He ran out to get a closer look.

"Hello there, little guy!" two nurses giggled.

"His name is Geronimo," I told them, "Nonnie is his **best friend**. This will be a **big adjustment** for him."

An adjustment? Geronimo thought. *Why do I need an adjustment?*

The family gathered around, "I am Ellie, and this is Emmy. We will be Nonnie's **nurses**, we will check on her often. You can call us any time."

Geronimo stayed close to Nonnie. He was concerned as Emmy took out a blood pressure cuff.

What is happening?

He wondered.

"Her blood pressure is good, but her **dementia** will get worse," said Ellie.

"You can expect **more changes**. Nonnie will soon forget things like how to make a cup of coffee, and she may not remember your names. It is important to have a lot of patience with her. Please call us if you need anything."

Everyone thanked Ellie and Emmy for their help.

Geronimo sat outside with Nonnie. She asked him **the same questions**

again

and

again.

He **sighed** as he remembered Ellie's words, *"it is important to have a lot of patience."*

Geronimo snuggled into his old bed, **ready for a long day**.

Our family took turns **caring** for Nonnie.

I shopped for food and took her to her doctors' appointments.

I cooked healthy meals...

...and helped her eat when she could no longer hold a spoon.

At night, when Nonnie could not sleep, Geronimo and I read to her, softly.

One morning, two men came to Nonnie's house with a new bed and **scary** machines.

The new bed had **railings** on the sides, just like a baby bed.

"WOOF! WOOF!"

*Why does she need a **baby bed**?*

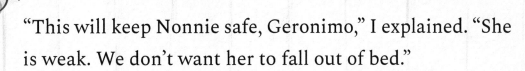

"This will keep Nonnie safe, Geronimo," I explained. "She is weak. We don't want her to fall out of bed."

"**WOOF!** **WOOF!**"

Geronimo barked. *No more changes!*

However, **many more** changes came.

Geronimo **snuggled** with Nonnie in her new bed.

He was careful near the wires and tubes. They brought medicine to her body.

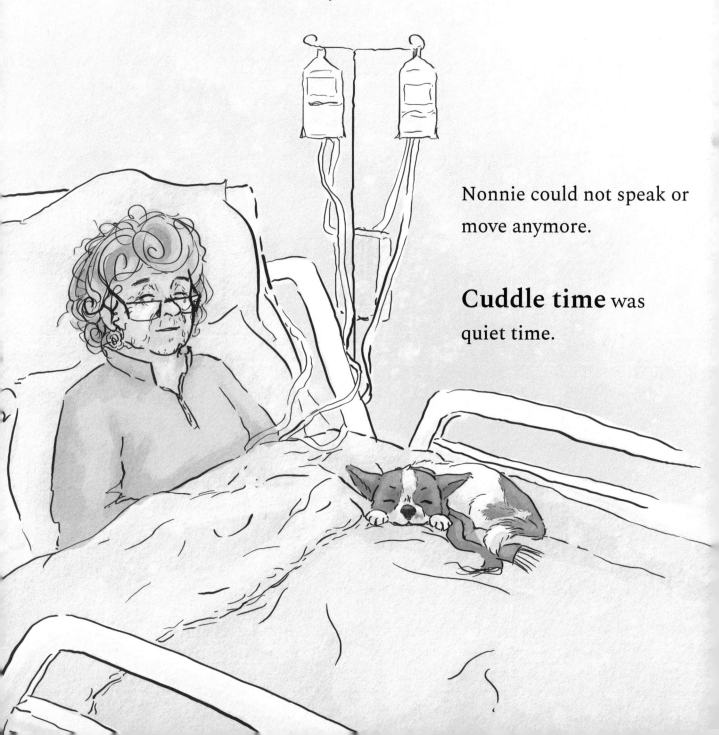

Nonnie could not speak or move anymore.

Cuddle time was quiet time.

One wintry day, while Geronimo kept warm by the woodstove, the phone rang.

"Hello? Okay, we'll be right over."

"Okay, little guy, we're going to see Nonnie. It's time to give her **one last kiss**."

Geronimo's heart was beating fast. *Last kiss?* He thought.

"WOOF!
            WOOF!"

he tried to tell them.

I have
a million more kisses
to give her!

Geronimo **ran** to Nonnie's front door.

He sniffed the air.
Something was **different**.

A breeze blew in through the open window
as Geronimo **lay down** next to Nonnie.
He squinted his eyes to the sun.

"Peep! Peep!"

The bluebirds called out to him.

"Caw! Caw!"

The crows cried.

Geronimo remembered Nonnie's words by the stream, "I wonder what they are trying to tell us?"

"**We are still here**," Geronimo heard them say.

"The wildflowers are still here. Audrey and the library are still here.

You will have fun again."

At Nonnie's funeral, everyone had special stories to share about her.

Geronimo learned a lot about Nonnie.

When someone needed a place to live, Nonnie would invite them to stay.

When someone came over for a visit, Nonnie would cook them a meal.

Geronimo realized he must be special for Nonnie to love him so much.

The long winter **passed**. Geronimo's tongue hung down as he lay in the sun. He missed Nonnie's wildflowers and the stream. He missed her **gentle voice** as she read their stories.

A warm breeze blew over Geronimo, and he **remembered** Nonnie's soft touch.

Instead of feeling sad, he allowed the beautiful **memories** to make him feel happy.

He realized that memories are a gift. A special **gift** left by someone who will **always love him**.

Geronimo talks about grief

When we lose someone we love, we say we have a broken heart. Sometimes we feel angry or scared, and sometimes we feel lonely. We call these feelings 'grief', and grief can hurt a lot.

There are ways to help heal our broken heart:

Even if we can't see our loved one, we can still talk to them. Close your eyes and whisper gently, or tell them a funny joke!

We can draw pictures of special times spent with our loved one.

We can talk about our loved one to others. What's your **favourite** story to tell?

If you know someone who is grieving, it is kind to reach out and try to help them feel better.

Geronimo wants you to remember:

Healing takes time.

When you feel sad, find your favourite part of nature and allow it to bring you joy.

Geronimo finds joy in this dragonfly!

First published in the USA in 2020 by Woody Knoll Publishing.

Text and illustrations © René Schultz 2020.

Author: René Schultz
Illustrator: Becky Stout
Designed by Stand Out Stories Ltd

The moral rights of the author and illustrator have been asserted.

All rights reserved. No part of this publication may be reproduced, stored in a retrieval system or transmitted in any form or by any means electronic, mechanical, photocopying, recording or otherwise, without prior written permission of the copyright owner.

ISBN: 978-1-7351560-4-0 (Hardback)
ISBN: 978-1-7351560-7-1 (E-Book)
ISBN: 978-1-7351560-0-2 (Paperback)

www.wknollpublishing.com

CPSIA information can be obtained
at www.ICGtesting.com
Printed in the USA
BVHW092056061020
590468BV00003B/4

HOOKSETT PUBLIC LIBRARY
HOOKSETT, NH 03106
603.485.6092
http://hooksettlibrary.org